# Oscar's Wings

*MUCKLEWOOD ADVENTURES*

# Oscar's Wings

**BRIAN CHALMERS**

RITCHIE
John Ritchie Publishing

40 Beansburn, Kilmarnock, Scotland

ISBN-13: 978 1914273 17 9


Copyright © 2022 by John Ritchie Ltd.
40 Beansburn, Kilmarnock, Scotland

**www.ritchiechristianmedia.co.uk**

Typeset by John Ritchie Ltd., Kilmarnock
Printed by Bell & Bain Ltd., Glasgow


Illustrations by Bethany McClean  @bmccleanart

To Ruthanna and her pointed and industrious
editing companion, Bic® Pen!

# Acknowledgements

My grateful thanks to Alison Banks, General Manager at John Ritchie Ltd., for suggesting that this work, previously published as a serial story for 'Our Treasury' children's magazine, be published as a book, Fraser Munro for his meticulous proofreading and helpful suggestions, Bethany McClean for bringing the scenes and characters of the story to life with her amazing illustrations and everyone involved in the production and marketing of this book.

**"Our soul is escaped as a bird out of the snare of the fowlers\*: the snare is broken, and we are escaped"** Psalm 124:7

\*Fowlers are people who catch birds in a trap or snare

# Contents

## Symbols used throughout the book

 Turn to the next page for the chapter application

*At the footnotes ...*

 A verse in the Bible to do with creation

 A verse in the Bible to do with us

 A verse in the Bible to do with the Lord Jesus Christ

 A verse in the Bible to do with the promises of God

 A verse in the Bible giving us instruction and warning

# Prologue

A frail form emerged from a hole in a tree to address another much larger, stronger bird than itself, perched on a branch near it.

"Go, Virtos; and may your journey bring the good news we hope for," the smaller bird said. "And remember, no one is to be trusted. Speak to no one," it cautioned.

Virtos sprung off the branch, and with its powerful wings, soared high into the sky until it found an agreeable altitude. Before long, like the ground mist below it, Virtos disappeared out of sight as the sun burst forth to greet the day.

# Oscar's Wings

# Chapter 1
# **Freedom**

Oscar stared through the dull pattern of wire mesh to the forest beyond, lit up dramatically by the moon. His so-called 'Owl Sanctuary', an enclosure small and featureless, was more of a prison than a paradise. Most of his days were spent thinking about freedom and flight; soaring high towards the stars on evenings like this one, and then dipping, swooping, skimming over the fresh and abundant ground on the other side of the wire.

Oscar, you may have guessed, was born in captivity, and was the illegal property of a man who cared more about the little profits he made from his collection of "exotic and rare birds" than for their welfare. The birds named him Miserly Shakes. He was tall, thin, and gaunt looking; rarely smiled (except when the donation box was full) and took pleasure in cruelty. In the early days, coach loads of enchanted visitors would give generously, thinking that the birds of Mucklewood Aviary would benefit. Back then the box was checked without fail on Saturdays - naturally the busiest day for visitors. He'd unhook the box from a fence post outside Oscar's enclosure and shake it close to his right ear before emptying the contents into a plastic bag to spend later, mostly on himself. That was his ritual - shake the box then empty its contents; earning him his unflattering nickname. His lack of care for the birds soon became apparent to visitors, and before long interest in his enterprise more resembled that of a trickling stream with starts and stops, than of a constant surging river. Sadly, as the aviary was visited less, the birds suffered more. Malnourishment and neglect resulted frequently in disease and premature death. At one stage it had over thirty birds, but now it had only nine.

Oscar was the last addition to Miserly Shakes' collection. And for the few visitors that did trickle in, this cute Northern Saw-whet Owl was the star attraction - sleeping or not!

There was one growing comfort for Oscar and his fellow captives however; from time to time a pair of Wood Pigeons, Sebastian and Charlotte, visited the compound to tell them of news from the forest. Most exciting of all, a plan had been formed to set them free. "Operation Flight" was to take place in the early evening hours of the next new moon, just a few weeks away.

# Freedom

This night, Oscar was visited by Sebastian alone. He knew instantly that something was wrong; the pair were inseparable.

"Where's Charlotte?" Oscar asked, fearing the worst.

"She's gone, Oscar!" Sebastian uttered in desperation.

"Gone? I don't understand. What do you mean, gone?"

The sudden thud of an outside door startled Sebastian away. Miserly Shakes was out for his nightly patrol of the compound with his less-than-charming dogs, Brutus and Shanks. With a flap of his wings, Oscar flew back to his branch and sat wondering about what Sebastian meant when he said that Charlotte was "gone" - there wasn't much else he could do. His eyes grew heavy until they eventually closed. The owls of the forest were just stirring as Oscar slipped into unconsciousness. He dreamed that he was gliding free in the wind and being borne higher and higher, far above the noise of farm machinery below. Sebastian and Charlotte joined him, and they flew together over the forest he'd always dreamed of living in. But that's all it was, for now at least - just a dream!

# Are you free?

Many years ago, I had a Zebra Finch called Cheeko. It was a cute little bird, but it did have an annoying habit of gnawing at the wire of its cage. I'm pretty sure it was trying to tell me that it wanted out. Now, in case you are wondering, I did let it out on occasion, but it was a total nightmare to get it back in its cage again. No sooner was it back in its cage than it was back to its gnawing habit again. Poor thing!

I think that our sins (the bad things we think, imagine, say and do) are a bit like a cage we wish we could escape from. But no matter how hard we try to break free from our sinful habits, even our best efforts are totally useless in the end. Worse than that, all sin is against God and separates us from Him. The good news is that the Son of God - the very One who created this universe* - left heaven and came into the world to set us free from our sins and to bring us into a right relationship with God. When Jesus died on the cross, He was offering Himself in our place for the punishment of our sins. Trusting in the Lord Jesus brings true life and **freedom**, and promises us heaven in a day to come.

**"Christ Jesus came into the world to save sinners."**
1 Timothy 1:15

* "In the beginning was the Word [a title of Jesus], and the Word was with God, and the Word was God ... All things were made through Him, and without Him nothing was made that was made ... And the Word became flesh and dwelt among us ..." John 1:1, 3, 14 (NKJV)

# Chapter 2
# **Dawning**

The next morning, the birds of Mucklewood forest commenced a full-scale search for Charlotte. About the same time, Miserly Shakes had sped off in his rackety old jeep, looking uncharacteristically purposeful, even bordering on cheerful. Glancing through the newspaper during breakfast, a headline had caught his attention. It read: 'Business Thrives After Renovation'. He understood instantly what should be done to save his enterprise from closure.

At the aviary, a neighbour to Oscar, a Shoebill Stork called Egbert, tried everything in his craft to stir Oscar out of sleep. After shrieking out his unique Shoebill call - sounding something like a machine gun firing a round of ammunition - he progressed to rattling a stick in-between a segment of the partition wire. The stick soon turned into

several twigs at Oscar's side of the fence. Finally, Egbert battered his metal bowl against a rock by his pool until it was rendered completely unfit for any purpose. Just as well he never used it! Exhausted and frustrated, his long cane-like legs buckled to the ground, and the hollow thud of his large bill on his chest announced that, to his great dissatisfaction, his efforts had concluded.

At that precise moment, like stage curtains falling upon one scene and rising upon another, Oscar's eyes gradually opened.

"There's a search going on for Charlotte," Egbert's voice droned.

Oscar moved his head, as owls do, and, distracted momentarily by an odd looking metal object in Egbert's enclosure, looked over to his eccentric friend, now poised in his pool for some hydrotherapy.

"A search you say! What happened to her?" Oscar asked.

"That's the problem," replied Egbert. "No one really knows. One minute she was foraging in the Walled Garden with Sebastian, and the next … well … Sebastian looked round and she wasn't there. Not even the sound of flapping wings. She had just vanished out of sight. Gone!"

"Really? That's most unusual!" Oscar offered.

A silence elapsed for a few moments whilst Egbert submerged his head under the water, pretending to hunt for fish.

"What if she didn't fly away?" Oscar suggested. "What if she was snatched away by a poacher, or something else?"

Egbert's signature stare was read perfectly by Oscar. It was saying that Oscar's bird-snatching theory was plausible.

The evening approached and the birds of the forest returned home after a fruitless search for Charlotte. During their absence, a band of Hooded Crows from Dark Moor had been menacingly encircling their territory for young birds. A new strategy would be determined in the morning to allow the search for Charlotte to continue whilst the young birds of Mucklewood forest were protected.

As night swept in, Oscar wondered if there was anything he could do to help with the search.

*"If only I was free!"* he thought. *"We'd find Charlotte, free the birds, and sort out that miserable Miserly once and for all!"*

Clouds covering the moon passed to reveal the waning gibbous. The new moon was approaching soon, but with the disappearance of Charlotte, Oscar now wondered if "Operation Flight" would ever take place. The strange, half-buried object in Egbert's enclosure bounced off light from the moon to Oscar's eyes. Suddenly, an idea dawned upon him.

"That's it!" Oscar announced to himself. He had thought of a way of escape from his enclosure to help in the search for Charlotte; but it would be risky. He flew off his branch and started about his plan. Time was of the essence!

# Commit your ways to God

Have you ever wanted to help someone or maybe fix a situation that had gone badly wrong, but you didn't know exactly how to go about it? Perhaps it was someone at school or in your neighbourhood who wasn't the easiest to make friends with, but you wanted to try and get to know them better. Or maybe a misunderstanding came between you and a close friend that resulted in your friendship with them ending. There you were, racking your brain, hoping for an idea to suddenly **dawn** upon you out of nowhere. But that idea never came, or the opportunity to carry it out passed. Maybe you even tried to do something and the problem was actually made worse! Yep, I've been there before! In every situation, it's good to take our concerns before God in prayer. He has all the best solutions and never grows weary of us asking Him for wisdom.

**"If any of you lack wisdom, let him ask of God ... and it shall be given him."** James 1:5

# Chapter 3
# **Plan**

"Egbert! Psst! Over Here!"

Egbert the Shoebill had been staring, as Shoebills do, but couldn't see Oscar anywhere.

"Over here, by the door, Egbert!"

Now looking around the door area of Oscar's enclosure, Egbert focussed upon a small mound of earth with an upside-down metal bowl, like his own bashed-up one in its former glory, tilted off one side of the mound.

"That's it, Egbert, I'm here! Can you see me now?" the familiar voice enquired.

Egbert saw two bright yellow rings just visible under the rim of the bowl.

*"Like eyes,"* Egbert thought. Until he realised they were!

Egbert opened his large bill in astonishment, to reveal an even larger mouth.

"How did you ... I mean, what are you ... I mean, why are you under there, Oscar?"

For a moment Egbert reasoned that Oscar had gone quite mad - moon-stroke or something like that, if there was such a thing!

"I'm going to help with the search for Charlotte," Oscar replied, his voice slightly muffled under the bowl. "And I'll be back with the others at the new moon."

Egbert looked as puzzled as ever, wondering how a half-buried bird would be of any use to itself, let alone Charlotte and the aviary, for all that.

Equally confused was an extremely shy Hoopoe bird called Maja. Most unusually, she ventured from her nest box towards the wire partition to the right of Oscar to, as best as she could, comprehend the situation.

"When I give the signal, Egbert, I need you to make as much noise and fuss as you can. That should alert Miserly Shakes. When he doesn't see me, he'll probably open the door to investigate. I'll fly out as soon as he passes."

Whilst Egbert thought about Oscar's daring plan, Maja, venturing to break another record in her entire time at the aviary, addressed Oscar.

"I'll help if you want me to," she said, directing her voice toward the pile of earth.

# Plan

Pleasantly surprised by Maja's suggestion, Oscar expressed his gratitude. Egbert just stared at Maja, expressing his gratitude in his usual manner.

Miserly Shakes was preparing a disused cabin to the rear of the aviary for the purpose of temporarily holding the birds whilst he made some improvements to their enclosures in a few days' time. For once, though with some reluctance and dither, he had decided to buy in a good stock of food for the birds with added vitamins. He wanted them to look their best for his relaunch of the aviary, which was planned for a week on Saturday - the day following the new moon. He was just about to break off for lunch when he heard frantic calls and shrieks from the birds of his aviary. What started off with Egbert and Maja, soon spread, and the rest of the aviary birds joined in, though most of them weren't sure exactly why.

Having checked on several enclosures, he stopped at Oscar's, and, as Oscar anticipated he would, unpadlocked the door and ventured in. Unknown to Oscar, Brutus and Shanks were waiting outside his enclosure. Miserly Shakes stepped past the mound where Oscar was hiding and was about to turn on himself to shut the door when Oscar, with all the might he could muster, leapt out from under the earth, thrusting the plate behind him, scattering dust into the air, conveniently irritating Miserly Shakes' eyes and obscuring his vision. Oscar soared for the sky beyond the door.

However, not expecting to see the two dogs at the door entrance, Oscar hovered in hesitation before flapping past Brutus. Shanks, by far the more athletic and agile of the two dogs, launched into the air and clipped Oscar mid-flight. Off-balance, Oscar hurtled uncontrollably to the ground.

By the time Oscar opened his eyes again, Shanks had him pinned down by his wings and Brutus was growling at him from another angle. It was the first time Oscar had seen the dogs up close, and they were much uglier and even less charming than he had previously thought!

# A plan that couldn't fail

Sometimes we make plans for things that just don't come to pass or that fail in the process of carrying them out. As a young teenager, I used to love planning bike days out with my friends. Sometimes these ended up in disaster: a flat tyre and no repair kit on one occasion, a broken leg on another! It's great to know that while our plans might fail, God's plans never have and never will! For example, when sin entered into the world because Adam and Eve (the first man* and woman) disobeyed God, this resulted in the relationship between the Creator and His creatures** being spoiled. But God already had a wonderful **plan** in place. Just at the right time, God sent His Son into the world to make available salvation from the consequences of our sins and to restore the relationship between us and our Creator that was lost when sin entered into the world. Many have come into the good of that plan by trusting in the Lord Jesus. How about you?

**"When the fulness of the time was come, God sent forth His Son ..."** Galatians 4:4

---

* "Wherefore, as by one man sin entered into the world, and death by sin; and so death passed upon all men, for that all have sinned." Romans 5:12

** "... God created man in His own image, in the image of God created He him; male and female created He them." Genesis 1:27

# Chapter 4
# **Folly**

On the day of Oscar's planned escape, the Hooded Crows of Dark Moor dispersed from the overcrowded clump of trees they reluctantly called "home" to hunt for food; some around Dark Moor itself and others further afield. One of the Hoodies was sidling and hopping, as crows do, near the opening of an old and disused oil chamber, just outside the walled garden of Mucklewood Estate. His curiosity was stirred by the faint but unmistakable call of a Wood Pigeon from within the chamber. Prying down through a gap created by the displacement of the chamber lid, into a tank as dark as his head, he proceeded to imitate the pigeon call as best and as convincingly as he could.

"Sebastian? Is that you?" replied a weak but hope-filled voice from the darkness.

"No!" the startled crow declared. "I'm not from these parts," he mimicked, pigeon-perfect. "I'm just flying through the area. Stopped for a breather. Just as well, eh?"

The bird in the chamber thought it necessary to be as precise and to the point as it could.

"Please, ... can you tell the birds of Mucklewood forest that I'm here; ..." requested the trapped bird, pausing briefly as it gasped for more air. "... that Charlotte is here?"

It was now two days since Charlotte had become trapped, and all she could think about was how foolish she had been to wander away from Sebastian outside the walled garden, allured by an object shining in the sun. Paying little attention to where she was walking, she had fallen down the hole where the hatch lid was displaced, knocking herself unconscious off an iron bar on the way down. When she had come to herself again, she had tried to fly back out of the hole, but some oil residue had transferred onto her wings, making it impossible for her to get air borne. She had managed to climb to an inner ledge, a little higher than the base.

"Tell them we have to ... we have to save Oscar and the rest of the aviary birds," Charlotte continued. "You have to tell them ... that we have to go ahead with the plan ... at the new moon ... whatever happens to me."

Charlotte had never forgotten her promise to Oscar's father. If it wasn't for him, she wouldn't have been alive. Oscar's parents came from a far country where their species was in danger. It wasn't long before the bravery of Oscar's father earned them acceptance with the birds of Mucklewood forest - Charlotte being one of the young chicks, at that time, who was saved by him from an attack by the Hooded Crows of Dark Moor. After some time settling into the forest, a poacher managed to capture Oscar's mother and sell her on to Miserly Shakes, complete with nest and eggs; but not without a vicious scuffle from Oscar's father! This left the poacher with life-long scars and Oscar's father with life-threatening injuries. Sadly, Oscar was the only chick to survive in captivity. As for his mother, after Oscar was old enough to swoop to the ground and feed himself, she was taken from him never to be seen again. Oscar was visited by his father until he became too weak from the injuries he suffered from the poacher. Before he left the forest, Charlotte and the birds of Mucklewood forest solemnly promised him they'd rescue his son. This promise extended to the other captives of the aviary, but Oscar was their first priority.

Realising the significance of the information Charlotte just shared, the young crow flew off without any reply or delay.

Charlotte hoped upon the kindness of this travelling "pigeon" to deliver her message instantly to her friends at the forest. But this heartless menace was on a straight course to Dark Moor, calling the Hoodies back with him as he went.

# Don't stay away

I hated being sent up the stairs to my bedroom when I had been a bit naughty - especially on a sunny day when I could have been outside playing with my friends. Instead, I was stuck in my boring old bedroom! And as I huffed and muttered under my breath of how unfair the world was to me, I knew deep down that sulking wouldn't achieve anything, that I was at fault, and that, until I admitted I had acted in a **foolish** way, the enjoyment to be had in the world outside the four walls of my bedroom, was not to be experienced. It's not easy being a kid sometimes - trust me, I've been there - but it's equally not easy owning up to your wrong doings - whatever age you are!

Even Christians may think, say and do things they shouldn't, and if not quickly confessed to God, will result in the enjoyment of their fellowship with Him evaporating like steam from a kettle. Better to acknowledge our sins before God and confess them at the earliest opportunity.

**"If we confess our sins, He is faithful and just to forgive us our sins, and to cleanse us from all unrighteousness."**
1 John 1:9

# Chapter 5
# **Search**

Among the birds of Mucklewood forest, no one was as delighted to see Oscar as Sebastian was. It instantly raised his spirits and filled him with the hope that, if Oscar could escape from captivity, then anything was possible, and that meant that Charlotte could be found! Only a matter of minutes before, Oscar was in captivity. Now he was free, sitting among a company of birds who were delighted to meet him in person, and equally as keen to know exactly how this happy affair occurred.

Oscar settled himself down, barely having caught his breath, to unfold the story of his escape from the aviary. Starting with how his escape plan was inspired from a bashed metal object in Egbert's cage, he went on to tell of being pinned down to the ground by Shanks, and how the shy, but daring and unpredictable Maja had pierced Shanks through the fence with her long pointed beak,

causing Shanks to hurtle forward onto Brutus, who in turn thought that Shanks was fighting with him over Oscar. Finally he told of how Miserly Shakes, still trying to remove particles of grit from his eyes from the dust Oscar had created, stumbled and tumbled over his two dogs, whilst Oscar flew off triumphantly - the birds of the aviary cheering him on!

As they listened intently to Oscar, their eyes were transfixed by his gestures of swooping, hurtling, tumbling, soaring, and every other action he managed to animate throughout the account.

As night fell and conversation gave way to tiredness, Sebastian showed Oscar to his new home which was already prepared for him in anticipation of his release. For once in his life, Oscar could rest his eyes in absolute complacency in the knowledge that if he should dream that night of the forest, as he usually did, he would awake to its breathtaking reality.

---

The next morning Oscar was charged with a sense of purpose.

"We have to get out there and search for Charlotte," he urged the others. "And this is how we must do it … ."

Oscar may have been caged his whole life with no experience in the wild, but it became clear to everyone before the sun had properly risen that morning, that he was a natural leader. Search groups were selected, briefed and dispersed, all from the charge of Oscar.

Oscar paired himself with Sebastian and went to the Walled Garden where Charlotte was last seen. After a thorough but fruitless search of the garden they ventured outside to inspect the perimeter.

Sebastian was approaching the old oil chamber, calling as he went. He even lowered his head down the hole where Charlotte was trapped, called for Charlotte without any idea she was there, and his call went unanswered. Charlotte, though conscious, and aware that Sebastian was calling for her, was too weak by now to respond. She resigned herself to the fact that she would never see him again. A small mercy, she thought, was that she was able to hear Sebastian for one last time. All she could do was close her eyes and sleep away, filling her thoughts with all the happy memories she had with Sebastian.

*"At least they got my message,"* Charlotte told herself. *"And Oscar will be saved."*

# Lost and found!

There are a couple of occasions I remember being lost from my parents when I was a child. One was on holiday abroad, and the other was on a shopping trip in the city of Edinburgh. On both occasions the fault lay with myself - allured by some trivial distraction (typical of me), I had wandered away from them! A search for me took place, and how glad we all were when I was found! The Bible tells us that we are all like lost sheep going astray*, wandering in this world without the Good Shepherd** - the Lord Jesus Christ. Aren't you glad that the greatest ever **search** and rescue mission that took place was when the Son of God came into the world to seek and save lost sinners like you and me? I certainly am! And when we trust in the Lord Jesus, He takes care of us down here until we are safe with Him in heaven in a day to come. Not one of His "sheep" will be missing!

**"The Son of man [the Lord Jesus] is come to seek and to save that which was lost."** Luke 19:10

---

* "All we like sheep have gone astray; we have turned every one to his own way ..." Isaiah 53:6

** "I am the good shepherd. The good shepherd gives His life for the sheep." John 10:11 (NKJV)

# Chapter 6
# **Discovery**

When the birds of Mucklewood forest got home from their latest search for Charlotte, another surprise awaited them, but not the pleasant kind they had experienced the previous day with the appearance of Oscar. Perched on a branch, near the top of an old Scots Pine where the birds generally congregated before they dispersed to their nests at night, was a huge dark brown bird with a golden tinged head, heavy and unforgiving yellow hooked bill, and legs that were feathered down to its sharp and foreboding talons. It resettled itself on the branch to reveal a set of very long and broad wings with feathers splayed at the tips like an elongated Victorian hand fan. Whatever it was (for the birds had never seen anything quite so majestic) they were in no doubt it was an extremely powerful bird, which posed a potential threat to them all - not just the young birds. To minimise confusion among them, they decided to give it a name. Joey, the Great Spotted Woodpecker (also referred to on occasion as Pickpecker because of his talent in lock picking) suggested the name "Big Brown Bird." Present circumstances considered, Joey's suggestion was agreed upon unanimously - a first for him!

———————————

Oscar had lingered behind in the grounds of Mucklewood Estate to carry out a night search. With his excellent night vision, he reasoned that he might just see something that was missed during the day to lead him to Charlotte. He soared high into the star-canopied heavens, flapping his wings rapidly to gain height and speed, then levelling himself to glide for a while - savouring every new sensation he'd been deprived of during captivity.

After scanning the Walled Garden, he flew over Miserly Shakes' compound. He considered stopping off by the aviary to update Egbert and give him and the others some assurance. Caution prevailed, and he declined the impulse, feeling it would be too risky - he'd only just got his wings after all!

From there he turned back for a last look of the outside perimeter of the Walled Garden. The moon was unobstructed this night and Oscar could see practically anything moving on the ground beneath him. A tabby cat was walking delicately, as cats do, on the top stones of a drystone dyke - clearly hunting for field mice or some other rodents, maybe even a young rabbit. A hedgehog was foraging through a heap of leaves recent winds had swept into a damp dark corner of overgrown vegetation - perfect for some tasty slugs!

Oscar noticed something highly reflective and swooped down to investigate. Unknown to him, it was the object Charlotte had been drawn to before her accident. On approaching the object, still airborne, something else captured his attention through the opening at the disused oil chamber. Light from the moon caught the form of something, then it disappeared. This continued in a rhythmic fashion, as though, whatever it was, was inflating then deflating - light from the moon catching it as it "inflated." Oscar now stood on the chamber lid and contemplated entering through the opening. He was small enough to fit comfortably through the hole as long as he could master his hovering skills. Deciding this required further investigation he gently fluttered his wings to position himself over the opening, then alternated his flapping to allow him to suspend himself whilst slowly descending into the darkness. In no time he came to a ledge where the mysterious "object" was lying, only to discover that a poor creature, much larger than himself, was struggling to get air into its lungs. Oscar then noticed it had a distinct white patch on its neck and stepped onto the ledge to get a closer look.

The smell of oil residue was so strong he could almost taste it. Oscar cleared his throat in the air-starved tank.

"Charlotte! Is that you?" he asked.

# The greatest discovery

What has been your greatest discovery? Some of you might find that question quite hard and tricky to answer. I remember very clearly the day I made my greatest **discovery**. It was the evening after a New Year many years ago when I came to Jesus Christ, by simple faith, and asked Him to forgive my sins and to be my Saviour. At that very moment, then a young teenager, I discovered the peace of God and the joy of having all my sins forgiven. There is nothing to compare with this in all the world! Have you made that same discovery? You know, I didn't realise it at the time, but when I trusted in the Saviour, it was just the beginning of a lifetime of discovering how wonderful God, His Word - the Bible, and the Lord Jesus Christ are. Even in heaven, God's children will never stop discovering new things about their wonderful Saviour. If you are a Christian, is getting to know more about the Lord Jesus your top priority?* He certainly deserves it to be, does He not?

**"... the unsearchable riches of Christ."** Ephesians 3:8

---

* "... I also count all things loss for the excellence of the knowledge of Christ Jesus my Lord, for whom I have suffered the loss of all things, and count them as rubbish, that I may gain Christ." Philippians 3:8 (NKJV)

# Chapter 7
# Misery

Miserly Shakes was as miserable as ever. Just when his plans for rejuvenating the aviary were rolling along nicely, Oscar, his star attraction, had escaped. He summoned his life-long acquaintance and companion bird poacher, Douglas Morrison (Duggie), for an emergency meeting at his cottage. Most of their morning was spent on the veranda scanning the forest through their binoculars, looking for Oscar.

"Nothing, Sherrit!" Duggie groaned, "Not a flick or a flutter!"

By the time they had ventured out that morning, some of the birds of Mucklewood forest had already departed in response to a call from Oscar at the Walled Garden.

"Remember that bird that helped us out the last time?" Duggie asked, referring to one of the forest birds.

"Yeh!" muttered Miserly Shakes, "Must have gone off the food I gave it."

"Pity!" remarked Duggie, "We could be doing with its help again."

"He's out there somewhere. I know it!" said Miserly Shakes, referring back to Oscar. By now his voice was competing with Brutus and Shanks who were droning and whining, as dogs do, looking for a late morning treat. For all Miserly Shakes cared little for anyone but himself, his two dogs were the exception. He raised his elbows from off the veranda fence, used as a support for his arms, and rested his binoculars on his chest.

"Ahh bother!" Miserly exclaimed, looking back at the forest with frustration as he followed Brutus and Shanks indoors. The three of them hobbled inside, each suffering an injury from their dramatic and humiliating episode at the aviary a couple of days past. Duggie lingered outside a while longer before being called in for a hot drink. He wasn't sure where or by what, but he had a strong feeling he was being watched from a distance.

———————

Egbert and Maja were getting on well with each other since Oscar's escape. Fortunately for Maja, Shanks' injury was inflicted so effectively and swiftly that she had time to retreat to her nest box without him knowing the cause of his wound. Egbert encouraged Maja to retell what happened from her viewpoint time and again. She hardly believed her own account of the hilarious and triumphant sequence of events. Egbert offered the odd audible cord of laughter - cackling somewhat with his unique Shoebill call, now sounding more like a round of fire from a seriously faulty machine gun. At times he shook his large head from side to side, enjoying Maja's additional embellishments of each retelling. Mostly, though, he just stared with his 'laughter stare'. Maja soon learned the subtle change in Egbert's eyes when he was doing a laughter stare, and that just set her off all the more; the more Egbert stared, the more Maja laughed, the more Egbert stared … .

The New Moon was just eleven evenings away, but now that one of their company had found freedom, eleven evenings were eleven evenings too long, especially for Egbert and Maja, who were situated at either side of Oscar's empty enclosure. The birds of the aviary all sensed that Miserly Shakes was up to something, with all his bustling about the last couple of days, and hoped that, whatever it was, it wouldn't hinder the success of "Operation Flight."

———————————

"Sherrit! Grab your binocs. Quickly!"

Miserly Shakes assumed that Duggie had spotted Oscar and slid over the floor, as you might imagine a first time ice-skater would do, but on a wooden surface and wearing slippers - his leg injuries were quite forgotten for now!

"Look over there, on top of that large Scots Pine. Do you see it?" Duggie's voice went high with excitement.

"Well I never!" exclaimed Miserly Shakes. "It's not? ... is it?"

"Oh yes, my old friend, it certainly is! Who'd have thought we'd have seen one of those in our lifetime?"

Miserly Shakes was riveted to his binoculars, staring in utter amazement at the creature before his view. Finally he lowered his binoculars and turned to Duggie, facing the scarred side of Duggie's face - courtesy of Oscar's father a number of months back.

"If we could capture it, think of the trade we'd bring in," suggested Miserly Shakes.

"My thoughts exactly. But I'd want a good share of the profits this time Rodney - at least forty percent," Duggie said. Duggie always used Sherrit's first name when he was serious about something.

Miserly Shakes bartered Duggie down to thirty percent. They both shook on it! Once more, Rodney Sherrit had lived up to the name the birds gave him!

# Tree talk!

You don't need to be a tree expert to know that the root of a fruit tree is usually hidden underground while the fruit hangs from the branches for all to see, and that the fruit exists because there is a living root. Also, if you plant a pear tree, it won't by some weird freak of nature produce tangerines! There is a law of nature at work - what you sow is what will grow. In the same way, sin is a root that is deep in the very being of every human, and the fruit of that root can often be seen outwardly in various ways, such as a selfish act, a lying tongue, a mean attitude, an unkind comment, a cruel act, etc. That's not to mention the sins of our imagination! The sins we commit often result in **misery** and harm to ourselves and to others, and because God is our Creator, we are answerable to Him for them.* And yet, God's Son was sent into this world by His Father to deal with the very root of our sins. After suffering for our sin on the cross at Calvary, God raised His Son from the dead after three days.** When we come to God, own up to our sin, and trust by simple faith in the Lord Jesus, we are "born again". God plants a new nature in our hearts and the Holy Spirit helps us to produce fruit for the glory of God!

**"The fruit of the Spirit is love, joy, peace, longsuffering [patience], kindness, goodness, faithfulness, gentleness, self-control."** Galatians 5:22-23 (NKJV)

---

* "God, who made the world and everything in it ... in Him we live and move and have our being ..." Acts 17:24, 28 (NKJV)

** "And when they had fulfilled all that was written of Him, they took Him down from the tree, and laid Him in a sepulchre. But God raised Him from the dead." Acts 13:29-30

# Chapter 8
# Hope

Oscar's call was heard from the direction of the Walled Garden. It was barely morning, but many of the forest birds were fully awake and alert - thanks to the presence of the large bird on the old Scots Pine.

Sebastian was first from the forest to join Oscar.

"She's down there, Sebastian," Oscar announced, directing Sebastian's gaze to the chamber opening, and curbing any excitement from the tone of his voice so as not to give Sebastian too much hope. "I managed to give her a little water through the night. It has helped, but Charlotte's still very weak."

Sebastian was clearly charged with emotion; his eyes welled up with tears and he could barely speak. Some of the other birds now gathered around, but only a handful. Many of the forest birds had stayed behind to keep an eye on the Big Brown Bird, particularly the stronger and more experienced in fight and flight among them, such as Joey, the Great Spotted Woodpecker, with his powerful drilling beak - a nasty piece of equipment when required for defensive purposes!

Sebastian turned to speak to the few who had joined them whilst Oscar went back down the chamber hole to give Charlotte a little more water, carried in a folded leaf from an evergreen shrub.

"She's here!" Sebastian said to the birds, his voice quivering a little, "And she's alive!"

Sebastian carefully approached the opening, tilted his head down slightly, and spoke some words of reassurance and hope to Charlotte, his lifelong partner. Charlotte muttered a few words back, but they were too faint for Oscar to make out, let alone Sebastian.

"How are we going to get her out?" one of the birds asked at length. It was the question that was burning on all their minds.

A few hopeless suggestions were offered before Oscar spoke, having emerged from the chamber again.

"If we could move the lid to let more air in that would be a start."

They all agreed it was worth a try, but Oscar was encouraged to attend to Charlotte - she required all the care and reassurances she could get. After he disappeared down the chamber, the others set about their task.

Several collective efforts were made to move the displaced hatch lid, but to no avail. One of their company, a Tree Creeper called Jeremy, noticed they had unwanted company. The Big Brown Bird was poised upon the rooftop of the Walled Garden tower staring down at them like a weather vane of doom and gloom. As discreetly as he could, and holding his nerve quite admirably, Jeremy alerted the others. Sebastian then warned Oscar, who was still down in the chamber.

"There's danger, Oscar," Sebastian said.

Before Oscar had time to ask what the problem was, Jeremy, who had hardly flinched from looking at the Big Brown Bird from the side of his eyes, suddenly shrieked out a frantic and far less subtle alarm call than he did before:

"Everyone! Looook ouuuut!"

The Big Brown Bird sprung from off the tower roof and with a couple of effortless flaps glided down towards them. The birds managed to disperse in time, all scattering from each other; clamouring and darting in all directions in an erratic fashion, as birds do. Oscar, sensing something was wrong, hopped deeper into the ledge for cover.

The Big Brown Bird swooped down to the chamber and, in an almost continuous motion, gripped the lid with his powerful talons and flipped it up in the air away from the chamber. Sebastian witnessed the bird's breathtaking feat, wondering if he had just hallucinated. They watched it fly off, out of sight, in the direction of the aviary.

A few minutes passed before the birds congregated again around the old oil chamber and beckoned Oscar out. They told him about the Big Brown Bird, having not mentioned it to Oscar since they first saw it themselves the previous evening on return to the forest after their search for Charlotte.

"If he is really as bad as you think, why hasn't he hurt anyone yet?" Oscar asked, "And why would he move the lid for us?"

"Maybe he wanted to show us how powerful he is," Jeremy offered, but proceeded to correct himself, "but that doesn't make any sense does it? We've not put up any resistance to him yet."

"Yet! … Really?" Sebastian said, the thought of any confrontation with it being altogether foreign. "No, I think he'd have grabbed one of us, not the lid, if you hadn't warned us soon enough, Jeremy."

Everyone agreed, apart from Oscar who remained unconvinced, but joined in their notes of appreciation to Jeremy.

Their attention turned again to Charlotte. After another brief visit by Oscar, he reported that her breathing had already improved with the influx of fresh air, and now that the lid was away from the opening, Sebastian could be with Charlotte for the first time since she went missing.

"Enemy or not," Oscar said, as Sebastian was about to descend into the chamber, "the Big Brown Bird has done us a great favour."

Sebastian couldn't deny that!

# It's hope - but not as you know it!

If I were to say to you: "I *hope* to get out of bed in time for a croissant for breakfast tomorrow," then you would be correct in thinking that there might just be a possibility that it wouldn't actually happen. A number of things could prevent that hope from turning into a reality. For example:

1. I forgot to set the alarm and slept in. By the time I got up, all the croissants were eaten!

2. The alarm clock did work, but I was so tired I kept pressing the snooze button! By the time I got up ... yes, you guessed!

3. The alarm clock did work and I got out of bed in time, only to discover that someone beat me to the last croissant!

This is usually how we use the word "hope" - something that may or may not happen that we want to take place. When the Bible talks about "**hope**", however, it is speaking about something that is certain.* Every true Christian can be sure about being in heaven one day: this is a wonderful "hope". In the meantime, one of the ways that Christians can show their love for their Lord is by telling others about Him. Bringing the message of hope from the Bible to those who need it!

**"The hope which is laid up for you in heaven ..."**
Colossians 1:5

---

* "This hope we have as an anchor of the soul, both sure and steadfast ..." Hebrews 6:19 (NKJV)

# Chapter 9
# **Return**

A week had passed since Charlotte's rescue, and to the delight of all the birds of Mucklewood forest, she had made a full recovery. Sebastian, with the help and ingenuity of Fran (a friendly Raven who was expelled from her flock for being "too nice"), had managed to lift Charlotte out of the disused oil chamber. To that end Fran had selected a bamboo hanging basket from her vast collection of disused odds and ends (acquired mainly from a local dumping ground) which she modified, as Ravens do, to serve as a winch.

Much had transpired in the days during Charlotte's recovery. The birds of the aviary were temporarily moved to the cabin Miserly Shakes had prepared, allowing him to get on with the aviary's necessary repairs and much needed face-lift whilst Duggie was tasked with observing the new feathered visitor to Mucklewood. This would allow him to set traps in strategic locations in and around the forest - hoping for its capture. There was one "slight" problem though - the bird in question hadn't been seen since Miserly Shakes and Duggie's first sighting of it. Neither, for that matter, had the birds of the forest seen it after the incident with the oil chamber lid - much to their relief!

As the week progressed, Duggie decided to lay bird traps, many of which he set at ground level in the forest not unnoticed by many of the birds there. In just a matter of days the aviary would be reopened. Time was running out, and Miserly Shakes was hoping that his luck wasn't about to run out too with regards to the capture of Oscar or the other bird he and Duggie had set their sights upon.

At Dark Moor, the Hooded Crows were also finalising plans. Information given by Charlotte to the young bird who tricked her into thinking he was a Wood Pigeon, resulted in the proposal of their most daring invasion plan yet, and incidentally earned the crafty informer the nickname - "The Young Pretender." Their leader, Starandoff, had given orders for the higher ranking members of the Hoodies to proceed as they had proposed for the evening of the new moon.

———————————

Earlier in the week, the Big Brown Bird - a Golden Eagle called Virtos - had returned from his visit at Mucklewood to his homeland in a far off mountainous region with expanses of woodland. In one of those expanses he came to a tree where a bird, partly hidden in the shade of its nest in an old Woodpecker's hole, had been waiting for him. The bird in the nest could tell by Virtos' approach that the news he bore wasn't as hoped.

Virtos perched himself on a branch shooting out from the side of the nest opening.

"No sighting of him, I'm afraid," Virtos said with dismay.

"Didn't anyone speak of his whereabouts?" replied the other bird, its voice toned with sadness.

"I hadn't to speak to anyone - remember? You suspect there's a betrayer in their midst."

The bird in the nest acknowledged the fact.

Virtos was about to retire to his mountain-edge nest when he ventured to speak, and wondered if he should bother.

"There was a curious incident or two during my visit. Probably doesn't amount to anything though!"

"Yes?" the other bird replied, encouraging Virtos to elaborate and praying it would yield some hope.

"Some of the birds of the forest were interested in an underground tank partly covered over with a heavy lid. They tried to remove the lid, without any success, and I

thought I'd do them a favour and flip it over before heading off by the aviary for one last look. They all fled when I approached - I suppose that's understandable - but there didn't seem to be anything in the hole, not that I could see anyway. As I said, it's probably nothing."

"You said there was a couple of things?"

"Well, that same morning, two men, like the ones you described to me before - one thin with long hair and the other with scars on one side of his face - were standing outside the cottage next to the aviary and studying the forest with their looking instruments. At length, the thin man and his two dogs went inside and were limping as though some misfortune had recently befallen them."

The other bird thought for a moment.

"You said that you checked the aviary before you returned. Were the enclosures occupied?" it asked, processing every new detail carefully.

"Yes, there were some. At the front, facing the forest, there was a tall bird with a strange looking beak to one side of an empty enclosure, and a colourful bird with a long beak, black and white wings and a long crown of feathers to the other side. There were a few other birds besides this dotted around in enclosures off either side of the front ones."

The bird in the nest peeked its head out from the shade.

"Get your rest, Virtos," it said purposefully, "tomorrow you're flying back to Mucklewood forest. And I'm coming with you."

Virtos could see there was no point arguing about it joining him this time round; though he doubted, in its present state, it would be able to keep up with him, perhaps not even manage the full distance. He flew to his nest in the crags for his greatly anticipated rest.

# Happy reunion day!

Isn't it a wonderful thing to be reunited with family and friends after a long period of separation from them, or even to see the joy that others have on such occasions? I've witnessed a number of reunions at bus stations and train stations when I used them to travel for my studies and for work, and it always made me smile inside. Sometimes I try to imagine the joy of the occasion when the Lord Jesus went back to heaven having been in the very world He had created* for over thirty-three years. Having finished the great work which He was sent to do, the Lord Jesus **returned** back to heaven again and took His place at God's right hand.** It's amazing to think that there is now a Man in heaven seated at the right hand of God! One day, it could be heaven welcoming you! That all depends on whether or not you have come to God through faith in the Lord Jesus Christ - the only way to heaven!

**"I am the way, the truth, and the life. No one comes to the Father except through Me."** John 14:6 (NKJV)

* "He was in the world, and the world was made by Him ..." John 1:10
** "I came forth from the Father, and am come into the world: again, I leave the world, and go to the Father." John 16:28

# Chapter 10
# **Promise**

The sun crept up the wooden panels of a rickety old cabin hut in Miserly Shakes' compound until it burst through its grimy windows and filled the bleak interior with such warm tones of diffused light that it seemed to be sending its own message of hope to the eight captive birds of the aviary crammed inside the four walls of this temporary holding place. It was the day of the new moon - liberation day! And more than even the promise made by the forest birds to return to set them free, Egbert, in particular, was not unmindful of the pledge made by Oscar. That to him was enough to dispel any invading doubts.

The feeling among the birds of the forest was a mixture of excitement and nervousness; of anticipation and apprehension. Their mission's success depended on every detail of Charlotte's carefully thought out plan being carried out with precision. Worryingly, there was one potential threat to the success of "Operation Flight" reported back to the birds of the forest by Jeremy the Treecreeper, who was tasked the day before with checking the aviary over. The renovated enclosures, now ready to be occupied again, had all their padlocks removed and a magnetic plate was fixed onto each doorpost which snap-locked the door when it came into contact with the metal frame of the door. The doors could only be opened again by a remote controlled key. In addition to this, Miserly Shakes had fitted them with tight springs to ensure that they shut behind him to prevent a repeat Oscar-inspired escape. All of this could amount to Joey the "Pickpecker" (whose task it was to pick open all the enclosure padlocks) being out of a job and in turn the mission being called off. They could only hope that the aviary birds were still in the padlocked cabin come the invasion, just hours away.

Something more sinister, however, had gone unnoticed by the birds of Mucklewood forest. In the undergrowth of their forest boundary, a despatch of Hooded Crows were lurking under the dense canopy of fern, spaced from each other to encompass the forest's entire periphery. The previous evening, this band of bothersome bandits had flown toward the forest before diving to the ground some distance away and advancing on foot, under the cover of darkness, to just beyond the forest edge. This was all accomplished successfully under the command of The Young Pretender - promoted up through the ranks in recognition of his efforts which led to the Hoodies' own present mission. Stage one was now completed flawlessly. Only two further stages had to be successfully executed before the forest would become the new permanent home of the Hooded Crows. The departure of the birds of Mucklewood forest to the aviary for "Operation Flight" would set in motion stage two of the Hoodies' plan, when a "runner" would fly back to Dark Moor to signal for their remaining numbers to join them. Their leader, Starandoff, would intimate their arrival at the forest with his familiar grating call, setting in motion the final stage of their devastating plan. Before any of the remaining birds of the forest knew what had hit them, an attack would be lunged from beneath and above. Resisters were to be destroyed, nests to be devastated, and captives taken and used as ransom for the forest the Hoodies so prized.

Presently, all was strangely quiet in the forest. Oscar was deep in sleep and had been since his return in the early hours of the morning. Since Charlotte's safe return, Oscar was enjoying his freedom to excess; exploring the amazing countryside around the forest as often as his little body and wings would allow him to day and night. He even ventured as far as the loch beyond the forest, where there were refreshing waters for him to drink from brooks flowing into the loch. Consequently, his wings were stronger than ever, his aerial skills were almost completely mastered, and his sleeps were much deeper than when he was in captivity.

Whilst Oscar slept, Sebastian and Charlotte were perched on a Beech tree at the edge of the forest looking contemplatively towards the aviary, which was only just visible through the fading ground mist. A rustle was heard coming from under the fern just behind the tree where they were sitting. Sebastian strained his neck to look in the direction of the noise, but observed only the slight movements of a strand of fern. A short while afterwards, this whole process repeated itself, but the noise was coming from a different spot further round. The fern was too dense for Sebastian to see anything under its camouflage without him investigating. Contemplating he would, Charlotte intervened. "It's nothing, Sebastian," she advised him, "and you're making me nervous. It'll be a hungry vole or something foraging in the undergrowth."

Sebastian turned and smiled at Charlotte, now aware that the last thing he wanted to do was give her any cause for concern - she'd had enough drama to last her a lifetime! They gently huddled together, as pigeons do, and dosed in the warming beams of the winter sun. As chance would have it - unknown to both pigeons - The Young Pretender, who deceived Charlotte, was just a few metres away from them.

# God keeps His promises!

Have you ever broken a **promise** or had one broken? It's very disappointing to let others down when you meant to keep your word or to be let down, isn't it? What's worse, is when a promise is made and the person who has made it has no intention of fulfilling it. Certainly, those who profess to be God's children should never be guilty of that! There is One who never breaks His promises and who we can totally rely upon*: the Lord Jesus Christ! He has promised heaven for all who trust in Him. One day He will come to take every *living* Christian home to heaven with Him and they will be gathered together with every Christian who has *died*. That's another wonderful promise He will keep! Perhaps you are reading this and you have not yet trusted in the Lord Jesus Christ as your Saviour and therefore are not ready for His return. Trust in Him now - without delay!

**"If I go and prepare a place for you, I will come again and receive you to Myself; that where I am, there you may be also."** John 14:3 (NKJV)

---

* "In hope of eternal life, which God, that cannot lie, promised before the world began." Titus 1:2

## Chapter 11
# Deceit

The noise of clonking, clanking, and the occasional spurting announced that Duggie was arriving in his pickup truck. Miserly Shakes had just finished feeding the birds, still held in the cabin, with a mixture of fish, dried insects, seeds, grain, fruit and berries all strewn across the cabin floor for them to pick through. The birds were bewildered by this once-in-a-lifetime marathon feast, now entering its eighth day. Egbert cautioned to the others to go easy: "Miserly Shakes could be fattening us up for his own bird feast," he said, taking upon himself the fatherly mantle. Some agreed with his theory - mainly the larger birds - others, like Maja who had come out her shell remarkably since her friendship with Egbert, thought it was a hilarious notion, and an Ivory-billed Aracari called Alfredo didn't care what the reason was for this fiesta of food, especially if he was to be freed, as they all anticipated, after dusk that evening. Before long, encouraged by the others, Egbert threw caution to the wind and devoured every last trace of fish on the floor.

Duggie slammed his truck door shut with a loud thud, almost as an introduction to the announcement he was about to make. "I've spotted him!" he declared excitedly. Miserly Shakes just walked past Duggie, acknowledging him in his usual way with the slightest hint of a nod.

"Who?" asked Miserly Shakes, now washing his hands under a cold tap in the cottage, "The eagle or the owl?"

"The owl, Sherrit! The owwwl!" Duggie repeated, with impatient excitement. "I saw him resting on a fence post when I was working at Brodie's farm yesterday, and I think I know how to capture him." He opened his hand to reveal a small tranquillising dart. "It carries some risk," he said, "but if my aim's good, it should do the trick."

"And if your aim's not good?" Miserly asked.

"Well … I think you know the answer to that," replied Duggie.

Miserly Shakes remained silent as he reached for the brown sauce in the fridge and squirted its remaining contents, with the most atrocious sound, from the bottle onto a slab of musty farmhouse bread. After closing the fridge door again his eyes fixed upon the leaflet they were using to promote the aviary opening day, attached by a fridge magnet from the RSPB - not that he ever was a member!

"Under the circumstances, Duggie, I don't think we've got a better choice - have we?"

––––––––––––––

The touristy village of Drumlachen, near Mucklewood, was expecting an influx of foreign visitors in two executive coaches with a number of their company avid bird enthusiasts. The tourists were to arrive for dinner at Drumlachen Hotel and stay on for most of the day following. A guide from Drumlachen named Heidi, a young history graduate who was fluent in Mandarin, was to accompany those wanting to benefit from her local knowledge and translation skills - which was handy for visitors to this part of the country, even if they were fluent in English! Attractions included: The Old Mill House, the Winter Gardens of Drumlachen Castle, and, with some reluctance and reservation on the part of village officials who proposed the list, Mucklewood Aviary! The aviary had been advertised to the locals as being "Under New Management" - a complete lie of course - and was promoted with flyers and posters bragging that it had undergone "extensive renovations." A picture of the "new" owner - Douglas Morrison - was plastered all over the village with the unfortunate caption 'View Rare Species' directly underneath. In the few days in which the marketing material was circulated, the tight-knit community of locals, amused by the slogan, frequently quoted it as a slur against Duggie and Rodney Sherrit. Jokes were made that the world would be a better place if that kind of "rare species" (referring to both Sherrit and Duggie) were to become extinct! Many in the village had first-hand experience of how deceitful they were, especially Rodney Sherrit - by far the craftier of the two.

———————————

"Sherrit, do you want a hand moving those birds back into their enclosures before I hunt for your owl?" Duggie asked.

"Aye! That would be helpful I suppose," Miserly Shakes replied. "Just let me take the dogs out for a quick walk, will you. I'll be back shortly."

# God knows the 'real' me

According to one dictionary, the word **Deceit** is explained as: 'keeping the truth hidden, especially to get an advantage'. It reminds me of the Cuckoo. This deceitful bird waits for an opportunity to lay one of its eggs in the nest of a different breed of bird when they are away from their nest. It steals one of the eggs from the host nest and lays its own in its place. The 'new parents' are none the wiser, and the Cuckoo mother has saved herself the time and effort of raising her own young. Have you ever acted in a deceitful way before? Pretending to be ill to get off school? ... Saying you were hungry, when you weren't, but didn't want anyone else to get that last scrumptious cake? ... Making up a huge sob story to gain the sympathy and friendship of others? To act in a deceitful way may fool others, but we can't fool God. He knows the real us, and nothing is hid from Him. God wants us to own up to our sinful ways* - not to try and hide our sins from Him. The fact is, we can't anyway! Only the Lord Jesus can make our hearts pure when we trust in Him. When a person becomes a child of God, their sins are forgiven and they are given a new nature that enables them to live for Him, including being truthful and transparent.

**"The heart is deceitful above all things, and desperately wicked: who can know it? I the LORD search the heart ..."**
Jeremiah 17:9-10

---

 * "I acknowledged my sin to You, and my iniquity I have not hidden. I said, 'I will confess my transgressions to the LORD,' and You forgave the iniquity of my sin." Psalm 32:5 (NKJV)

# Chapter 12
# **Mistake**

Out of breath and covered from head to foot in mud, Miserly Shakes returned from walking his dogs - Brutus by his side and Shanks following at a distance with his tail and head pointing down. Miserly Shakes was walking rigidly and looked like a monster from planet Mud.

"Whaaat happened to youuu?" Duggie exclaimed, trying hard not to laugh.

"Argh! That daft dog - that's what happened to me!" grumbled Miserly Shakes, referring to Shanks. He squelched past Duggie to the outside water tap at his cottage.

It transpired that the tabby cat Oscar spotted the evening after his escape had been seen by Shanks and instantly pursued. Shanks had now recovered from his injury from Maja and couldn't resist chasing the cat. When Shanks wouldn't respond to the whistle blow, Miserly Shakes had run after him, limping on his right leg like he was running a three-legged race. Having gathered quite some momentum up a gentle-sloping hill, he had tumbled down its opposite not-so-gentle-sloping side, straight into a swamp of mud waiting for him at the bottom.

"Just leave the birds just now, Duggie. We can sort them tonight, or I'll easily move them myself tomorrow morning. You'd best be off and see if you can get that owl. Maybe check your traps first - you never know what you might find. Bah!"

Needless to say, Miserly's misadventure favoured "Operation Flight" in the most timely fashion: Joey the "Pickpecker" had only now one lock to pick!

---

"Ohhh! ... I'm stuffed to the gills!" declared Alfredo, the Ivory-billed Aracari. He was slouched on the cabin floor leaning against one of the walls like he had been left there by a hurricane.

"You'd better hope you're fit for take-off tonight, Alfredo," Egbert half-jested. The others laughed, but Alfredo was in too much pain from overeating to return a counter-quip.

Maja was perched on the cabin window, only managing to stand sideways on its narrow ledge, looking out at the forest.

# Mistake

"When I get out of here," she said wistfully, "I'll nest in a tree at the other side of the forest, looking in the opposite direction from this depressing place."

"Oh, the view on the other side of the forest is magnificent, just mag-nif-ic-ent," contributed Echo the Nightjar. "I lived in the heathland there … just beyond the forest … before my capture that is … yeees," she continued on. "It stretches down to a loch rich with fish … with fish, I say", directing that particular remark at Egbert, "and the flies, oh the flies at summertime … mmm … I can taste them now … of every variety you could think …"

"Oh dear!" interrupted Maja, preventing the others from falling into a trance with Echo's soft-spoken voice and long drawn out words, "Oh dear, oh dearie me!"

"What is it?" asked Egbert curiously, snapped from the brink of unconsciousness.

"Looks like poor Miserly Shakes has had an unfortunate accident," she said, beckoning the others over. They required no further encouragement!

In no time, all the "conscious" birds were up at the cabin window. Some only managed to jump up and down on the floor, fluttering their wings a little to catch brief glimpses of the amusing sight. Smiles soon turned into laughter, which turned into chuckles, cackles, roarings and convulsions of laughter; apart from Alfredo, that is, who was now fast asleep.

––––––––––

Sebastian and Charlotte were about to leave the Beech tree to ask Oscar to call everyone involved in "Operation Flight" for a final meeting before its commencement. Oscar's unique owl call commanded attention, and with an ever-growing respect among the birds for his marvellous exploits to date, the few less motivated birds also responded well to him.

"Did you ever get the name of that pigeon who passed my message on when I was trapped in the oil chamber?" Charlotte asked. Sebastian looked profoundly confused.

"What pigeon? And what do you mean? It was Oscar who found you by himself. No one told him about your whereabouts. Didn't he tell you that?"

It took a few moments for Sebastian's words to sink in before Charlotte realised she may have made a serious mistake in telling the "pigeon" of the forest birds' plan.

"No, Oscar didn't say," replied Charlotte. "At least I can't remember Oscar telling me. Well, I mean … he may have, but I wasn't taking much in at that stage."

# *Mistake*

"Then, whoever this stranger was, you're sure it was a pigeon? You did see it, right?" Charlotte didn't need to answer - her face confirmed Sebastian's worst fear.

Eavesdropping from a short distance away under the fern, The Young Pretender could hardly believe what he was hearing. *"I must do something about those pigeons,"* he thought to himself, *"and fast, before word gets back to the other birds and we lose the element of surprise. Maybe even get discovered beforehand."* The fern rustled again. Sebastian hesitated to look behind him.

Swwwish!

# Don't be mistaken!

It's common to make **mistakes** about many things in life. Have you ever mistaken a space satellite for a star, or a jug of gravy for a jug of toffee sauce, or a lamb for a Poodle? "Yes," you say, "but not the last two." Fair enough! How about mistaking the identity of a stranger for someone you thought you knew? It's really easy to do that, and it can end up being quite embarrassing. One thing we can't afford to make any mistake about, however, is God's true identity! People have all sorts of wrong ideas about God and His Son - the Lord Jesus Christ. By memorising key verses of the Bible and being in the habit of reading our Bible daily (and going on to study it as we grow), we'll be able to give a defence of the Truth and explain why we believe what we believe from God's Word\*. If we don't, the danger is that we may believe everything we hear. We can think of our Christian life like the building of a house. Having a good foundation for a house is important, but so too is the need to build on that foundation using the correct materials. God's Word is not only a sure foundation to build our lives upon, but it is the building blocks and mortar for the whole structure. Without it, our ideas will easily blow away, like a house made with nothing but straw.

**"Be diligent to present yourself approved to God, a worker who does not need to be ashamed, rightly dividing the word of truth."** 2 Timothy 2:15 (NKJV)

---

\* "... always be ready to give a defence to everyone who asks you a reason for the hope that is in you, with meekness and fear." 1 Peter 3:15 (NKJV)

# Chapter 13
# **Alarm**

The Starlings were tolerated by the birds of Mucklewood forest because, although they were greedy and moody and loud and frequently fell out among themselves, let alone with everyone else, they offered the forest a level of protection and, most importantly, they absolutely hated the Hooded Crows and weren't afraid to show it. They roosted all around the outer trees of the forest and were given this privilege in return for the odd favour. One such favour was required of them in just a few hours' time, when they would be used as a decoy to help in the rescue of the captive birds of the aviary.

Miserly Shakes was all cleaned up from his mud swamp incident and enjoying a hot drink on his armchair, the flames of his open fire putting him into a trance. Brutus was snoring heavily by his side, as Bulldogs do, and Shanks was left whining outdoors in the freezing cold kennel grounds

as punishment for his most recent episode with the cat. Suddenly, as if an electrical current had surged through Brutus' body, he rose to his feet - in the most clumsy manner - and scampered on the wooden floor until he stood barking and frothing at the front door. Fortunately for Miserly, his cup was only a quarter full when his whole body jerked with fright and its contents sizzled in the fire. Approaching Brutus, about to cuff him on the nose, Miserly Shakes could hear the sound of various birds shrilling and squawking - the Starlings and Crows being the most pronounced. He went outside to the veranda and saw a huge murmuration of Starlings, whirling and darting, wheeling and swooping in sequenced patterns, encircling the forest. The forest looked like it was wrapped in one gigantic black bin liner fluttering in all directions in the wind. Then, emerging out from the chaos, Miserly could see Duggie through his binoculars. He was wrestling his way through some shrubs and shambling over the fern before he darted as fast as he could (which wasn't very fast) away from the mayhem of the forest towards Miserly's cottage. Puzzled and slightly bemused, Miserly Shakes took some comfort from the fact that he wasn't the only one to suffer some upset that day.

———————

Not long before this, when Sebastian and Charlotte had noted the mysterious rustling in the ferns, they felt something dart behind them. Whatever it was, it was gone by the time they both decided to turn round. Everything in the forest looked undisturbed again, but not for very long! With The Young Pretender absent without any warning to his comrades, the Hooded Crows at eyeshot either side of him began to panic. Before long this panic spread, until, like soot-covered popcorn popping up all over the place, the dark heads of the Hooded Crows emerged from beneath the fern, exposing their presence to the birds of the forest. In no time, the forest awoke with shrieks of alarm and the Starlings employed their "Lockdown" strategy most effectively - surrounding the forest perimeter to prevent intruders from escaping. The "runner" for the Hoodies was positioned just outside the forest. Upon hearing the commotion and seeing the forest surrounded with myriads of Starlings, he flew off to Dark Moor to inform the others. With nowhere to escape, the Hooded Crows were flying all over the place haphazardly. Some of their numbers tried to find cover again in the undergrowth, but it was no use, they were too outnumbered; eyes and wings followed them wherever they went. The birds of the forest interchanged turns to allow some rest in-between chasing the Hoodies as they were hounded to exhaustion.

# Alarm

Oscar came up with the most effective tactic of capturing the Hoodies, which inspired even the young and smaller birds to join in. He had observed the location of every trap which Duggie had laid on the forest floor. With this in mind, Oscar flew in the path of a Hoodie and allowed it to pursue him until he came close to a trap, at which point he suddenly swerved upwards, leaving his less agile pursuer to fly straight into the trap. In the space of twenty minutes since the whole forest commotion began, every trap was full of Hooded Crows. Their remaining numbers were too exhausted to do anything but surrender. The traps were unpicked by Joey the "Pickpecker", and they were all taken and held at a deserted Badgers' sett until it was determined what should be done. A large company of Starlings were given charge over them.

Once the forest was secure again, Oscar called the birds of the forest to the old Scots Pine for Charlotte's address. Charlotte was perched on one of the lower branches and Sebastian and Oscar were sitting together on a branch adjacent to her.

"Despite what has happened today 'Operation Flight' will go ahead," she said. "In fact, due to present circumstances and the possibility of the remaining Hoodies of Dark Moor coming upon us soon, we're going …"

WHOOOOSH … THUMP!

Thrust down from the sky and lying on the ground in front of the old Scots Pine, was a Hooded Crow from Dark Moor.

"I'll tell you anything! Anything! Please, just don't hurt me," yelped the terrified bird - his eyes closed tight and his wings flapping about in the earth as it lay on its back. The Young Pretender had returned again to the forest, but not this time by choice!

# Act now!

Alarm sounds are unpleasant for a reason - they are designed to alert us, not to please us! An **alarm** calls us to act upon it. Whether it's the annoying chime of an alarm clock that tells us it's time to get up and prepare for the day ahead, or the blare of a train horn to warn us that it's approaching and we need to stay clear of the platform edge, or a fire alarm which urges us to exit the building as quickly and safely as we can. The message of the Gospel* (this word in the Bible means 'good news') also acts like an alarm, warning people that they need to turn from their sins and trust in the Lord Jesus Christ if they are to be saved from the judgment of God upon them. We've mentioned the importance of trusting in the Lord Jesus a number of times, but you may be asking yourself: "What does that actually mean?" It means that you *agree* with God about your sin - that all sin is against God and separates you from Him. You *accept* that Jesus is the Son of God. That He is the only way to heaven, and that His death on the cross and His resurrection is the answer to your sin. You *act* upon this knowledge, by confessing your sin before God and receiving Jesus as your Saviour and Lord of your life. Are you trusting in the Lord Jesus? Better to act upon God's Word now, than to leave it until it is too late.

**"Behold, now is the accepted time; behold, now is the day of salvation."** 2 Corinthians 6:2

---

* "And He [Jesus] said to them [the disciples], 'Go into all the world and preach the gospel to every creature.'" Mark 16:15 (NKJV)

# Chapter 14
# **Kindness**

A sparrow was enjoying some late afternoon rays of sun when the presence of an owl announced its arrival by perching itself on the pylon cable next to it.

"Don't be alarmed," the owl said to the petrified sparrow. "I'm on my way to Mucklewood forest. Do you know in what direction it is, and how far?"

The sparrow could barely speak at first and pointed with one of its wings in the direction of Mucklewood.

"It's not that far from here. What do you hope to find there?" asked the sparrow nervously.

"My son!" came back the brief reply.

"I doubt you'll make it before the sun goes down," said the sparrow, "but I don't suppose the darkness will be a great hindrance to you."

"No, but these things are," said the owl, lifting up his wings. "They have hindered me a great deal so far. I was flying with my friend, but he had to go on without me. I don't suppose you've seen a large golden feathered bird passing this way? You'd have noticed him if you did," remarked the owl.

"Afraid not."

A silence lapsed for a brief moment before the sparrow asked the owl about his wings.

"They were damaged some months back at Mucklewood by a cruel man," the owl said, referring to Duggie the poacher. "He managed to take my dear Rose and her clutch of eggs, and gave them to a man the birds of the forest call Miserly Shakes. Only one of our brood survived."

The sparrow sensed his great sadness and immediately changed the focus to the surviving owlet.

"What's its name?"

"Rose named him after me," said the owl. "His name is Oscar. I'm hopeful that he's still alive, and I'm on my way to Mucklewood to search for him."

"You left Oscar at Mucklewood with his mother?" enquired the sparrow.

"Rose was in an enclosure with Oscar for some weeks after his birth and then one day when I went to visit them both, as I did twice daily - before sunrise and after sun set - she wasn't there. I assume they sold her to a new owner.

"When I could no longer fly because of my injuries, I decided I wouldn't be a burden to the birds of the forest. A kind pigeon called Charlotte promised me that she, with the help of the other birds of the forest, would rescue my son, so I slipped away in the night in search of somewhere to burrow and pass away quietly; happy in the knowledge that one day young Oscar would have his own life with friends that would care for him like family."

"But you survived! How come?" the intrigued sparrow asked, now completely relaxed in his presence.

"Well, I did find a little hole to burrow in, but a dog sniffed me out the next morning and its kind owner took me up, carried me away - far from Mucklewood - and nurtured me until I was in good health again. Eventually, I had got my wings back - I could fly! Not as once I could, you'll understand - flying takes a lot of effort for me now.

"I suppose the forest birds think me dead long ago; at least, they couldn't have thought I'd survive long after I left them, and they were none the wiser as to what happened to me."

The sparrow sat intense with interest and beckoned the owl to speak on.

"One day, the kind human let me free and I was fortunate to find a home in a near mountain range where the birds were as kind to me as those of Mucklewood forest had been - especially Virtos, the bird I started on this journey with."

With that, the owl thanked the sparrow for his help and recommenced his journey north-east towards Mucklewood.

# Undeserving love

It's natural to love those that love us, but what about people who are unkind to us? Not so easy, eh? God's love is totally different from human love. God loves us despite the fact that we have all disobeyed His commandments and have gone our own way in this life without Him. How **kind** it was of God to send His Son into a world He knew would eventually put Him on a cross to die in shame and agony. But we shouldn't think that the death of Jesus on the cross was an accident. The Old Testament scriptures foretold His death and Jesus often told His disciples that He was going to die and suffer for the sins of the world, and that He would be raised from the dead after three days. Trusting in the Lord Jesus, we can have our sins forgiven and be brought into a right relationship with God.

**"For God so loved the world that He gave His only begotten Son, that whoever believes in Him should not perish but have everlasting life."** John 3:16 (NKJV)

# Chapter 15
# Courage

"What do you think it's trying to tell us?" asked Duggie. He and Miserly Shakes had been visited by one of the forest birds.

"Whatever it is," said Miserly, "I think it's to do with our runaway Owl."

Miserly Shakes gave the bird another dead chick and off it flew again, repeating what it had done twice already: flying to the forest, then directly from there to Oscar's old enclosure, then to the cabin where the captive birds were being held.

"Oh, I see! I get it now, you clever bird!" said Miserly Shakes, taking the last dead chick out of a bucket. The bird stashed it away with the other dead chicks it received in a hiding place just outside the forest. Duggie was still none the wiser and was more interested in his squashed ham and pickle sandwich he had retrieved from his jacket

pocket, seasoned with some pine needles from his brush with the forest earlier.

"Oh, it's a clever one, Duggie!" said Miserly, "It's telling us about the Owl. Something to do with it visiting the cabin."

"Do you really think so?" muffled an unconvinced Duggie through a barricade of food in his mouth.

"I do indeed," insisted Miserly Shakes. "It led us to the Saw-whet Owls the last time, and, as sure as eggs is eggs, it wants us to capture our little feathery wanderer and have him back here where he belongs. Tell you what, Duggie, get your blow gun and darts. I'll put the dogs in the cottage and we'll shutter the kennel window and make a spy hole. If he visits the cabin tonight, you'll get a good shot from there."

———————————

At the forest, The Young Pretender, still suffering aftershock from his encounter with the mysterious bird who swept him up, ruffled him about, and thrust him down to the forest floor, revealed every single detail of what the Hooded Crows had set out to do regarding their invasion. Naturally, the forest birds were all keen to know who was responsible for capturing and depositing him, resulting in the next stage of the Hoodies' dark plan being thwarted. All The Young Pretender could tell them was it was big, fast and very strong, for his eyes were closed for most of the ordeal! The forest birds decided that their prisoners were to be held captive until "Operation Flight" was accomplished and all involved in the mission had returned back safely. The hope was to complete the mission before the remainder of the Hooded Crows of Dark Moor would arrive.

With time against them, Charlotte commenced where she had left off, addressing in particular all the birds involved in "Operation Flight".

"As I was saying, we're going to have to act sooner than planned. Let's go over the plan one more time: Fran! ... Fran! ... Does anybody know where Fran is?" Charlotte's question was met with silence. "Okay, she'll hopefully join us soon. Let's see ... who's next? ... Oscar!"

"After Fran returns from Miserly Shakes' compound," Oscar said, "I'll fly with Jeremy and hold back at my old enclosure while he checks the dogs are sleeping, or turned away from looking in the direction of the cabin. Once the all-clear is given, I'll approach the cabin to let them know that 'Operation Flight' has commenced and to get set to leave. I'll then return back here."

"Thanks, Oscar. Now …"

"I'm here! I'm here! Sorry I'm late!" announced Fran, interrupting Charlotte as she was about to ask Harry the Starling to speak. At Fran's feet lay a homemade thingamajig made from her vast collection of scrapped bits and bobs.

"Where have you been?" asked Charlotte.

"Sorry, sorry! Really, really sorry! I was just getting my light blinder for the mission," she said, referring to the object at her feet. "Forgot to pick it up on my way here at first and had to go back," she explained.

"We're going over the operation one last time, Fran," informed Charlotte, prompting Fran to recount her part in it.

"I've to go to the compound and drop my light blinder over the light outside of the cabin. Then I'll return to let Jeremy and Oscar go."

"Good!" said Charlotte. "So, to be clear, Fran first, then Jeremy and Oscar, then Harry and his team after Oscar's return. Now, Harry, if you could make it brief that would be appreciated!" requested Charlotte.

"Ahem! At Oscar's return, I and my elite team will go to the cottage and …"

"QUIETLY," interrupted Charlotte.

"Sorry, am I speaking too loud?" asked Harry, looking totally put off.

"No, I mean, you've to go to the cottage QUIETLY - remember?" (Starlings are notoriously unquiet.)

Harry cleared his throat again, this time to cover his embarrassment.

"Oh yes, of course. We shall proceed QUIETLY from the forest to the rooftop of Miserly Shakes' cottage where we will wait there QUIETLY. If Miserly Shakes comes out of his house during the mission we shall stop being QUIET and make as much noise and fuss as we can, which, as everyone knows here, we ..."

"Thank you!" intervened Charlotte. "Nearly there. Now, Joey please!"

Joey the Woodpecker stepped forward into the path of the fading sun. His silhouette was pronounced like some great hero just about to emerge from the shadows.

"Once the Starlings are in remission, em ... I mean position," he said, "I will go to the cabin roof, get the all clear from Jeremy, then pick the cabin lock. I'll then escort the birds to the boundary gate where Charlotte and Sebastian should be ... I mean will be. Definitely will be!"

"Super! Sounds like we're almost set," said Charlotte, with a slight tremor in her voice. The gravity of the task ahead was finally hitting home to her.

"Sebastian and I will wait at the boundary fence. Everyone else is to wait nearby in case you are required for backup," instructed Charlotte.

As the sun slipped away, the moon was in complete darkness. "Oscar will guide us safely back," Charlotte said reassuringly.

Fran picked up her "light blinder", waiting for Charlotte's word.

"It's time to do this!" Charlotte said, her voice now firm with courage. "Off you go, Fran!"

# Be courageous!

Fear is a terrible thing. It can make us act in a way we usually wouldn't act or stop us from saying something we know we should. Have you ever wanted to speak to someone about how you don't like it when they use the Lord's Name as a swear word, but you didn't say anything because you were afraid? Fear can swallow us up if we allow it to, but when we ask God to help us overcome our fears, He can give us the **courage** to overcome them. As for courage, many great things have been done for God by those who have dared to take their stand for Him. There are plenty of examples of this in God's Word*, but can you think of anyone you know today whose faith and courage are inspiring to you? No doubt there are many acts of faith and courage which are only known to God. Anyway, supposing nobody comes to your mind, all the more reason for you to take your stand for God, and with His help, to have the Lord honoured and maybe even other Christians encouraged and inspired by your example.

**"Be strong and of good courage; do not be afraid, nor be dismayed, for the LORD your God is with you wherever you go."** Joshua 1:9 (NKJV)

---

 * Some examples are: Joshua (Joshua 1), Deborah (Judges 4), Hannah (1 Samuel 1:1-18), David (1 Samuel 17), Esther (Esther 4+5), Daniel's three friends (Daniel 3), Daniel (Daniel 6), Peter (Matthew 14:22-33), Paul (2 Timothy 4:14-18)

# Chapter 16
# **Expectation**

Egbert had been pacing up and down the full length of the cabin, which wasn't very long - especially for a bird with long legs. Suddenly, he stopped in his tracks, looked up at the ceiling and stood as still as a statue with one of his legs bent in mid-air like a Flamingo. For a moment, Maja supposed he was doing some odd ritual thing that Shoebills do every once in a while.

"Do any of you hear that?" Egbert asked.

Alfredo the Ivory-billed Aracari was fully awake from sleep now, as was his appetite again.

"Oh, I do hope it's more food arriving," he said. "I'm as hungry as a hedgehog out of hibernation."

"We've yet to get a food delivery through the roof," remarked Fuzz the Frizzle chicken.

"Shhh! Listen!" commanded Egbert, "Something's on the roof. I'm sure of it."

Sure enough, they could hear the footsteps of what sounded like a medium to large-sized bird, walking and hopping on the cabin roof. It stopped at the cabin floodlight before they heard the clinking of metal against metal. In a few moments after this, it was heard flying off.

"This is it!" exclaimed Egbert, flapping his wings and shaking his head from side to side in excitement. "'Operation Flight' has commenced!"

The atmosphere in the cabin turned ecstatic. The birds were doing what birds do when they're happy - a lot of flapping and fluttering, chirping and chattering (or hollow bill clapping in the case of Egbert), and generally creating a scene of, what could only be described as, joyous mayhem.

"Anything?" asked Miserly Shakes. He and Duggie were in the kennel opposite the cabin. Duggie was looking at the cabin through the spy hole.

"Nothing yet," sighed Duggie. "The cabin's alive enough mind you. Those greedy gannets must be looking for more food - they're flying about frantically!"

"The light sensor will pick up movement outside," said Miserly Shakes. "We'll know of his presence alright," he continued, referring to Oscar.

Jeremy had just taken position on the kennel roof and decided to check on the dogs. As they were not out on the kennel grounds, he assumed they were inside their kennel. From the top of the kennel window frame he hung upside down, as Treecreepers do, but instead of looking through a wire-mesh window, as he'd expected to, he was confronted with a solid sheet of wood placed over the window!

"*Strange! Well, at least if we can't see them,*" he thought, referring to the dogs, "*then they can't see us!*" With a soft call, Jeremy gave the all-clear for Oscar to approach the cabin.

"Did you hear that?" asked Duggie, still looking out the spy hole.

"What?" asked Miserly Shakes.

"Sounded like a Treecreeper," said Duggie.

"A Treecreeper! Here! At this time of night!" scorned Miserly Shakes.

Suddenly Duggie could just make out the form of a bird at the outside of the cabin.

"Strange the light didn't come on, but there's a bird at the cabin window," he said, trying to focus in on it. After a few seconds, he was able to identify it. "Would you believe it, Sherrit? - it's the Saw-whet Owl," he gasped.

# Expectation

Duggie put the loaded blow gun in his mouth and slipped it through another hole specially made just underneath the spy hole.

"Easy does it ... ," he whispered to himself. Phhh ... zipppp ... doeff! "Ahh! I missed it!" exclaimed Duggie, in bitter frustration. The yellow-feathered end of the dart was seen in one of the cabin panels to the left side of the window.

"It hasn't noticed though!" Duggie added, much to Miserly's relief. Duggie quickly loaded up the blow gun with another tranquilliser dart. Miserly Shakes leant forward and sat rigid and tense on his camping chair, hoping that Duggie's second attempt would be successful.

To the delight of the birds inside the cabin, Oscar had tapped on the window to indicate that "Operation Flight" was going ahead. He was just about to leave, when ...

Phhh ... zippp ... shriek!

"Did you get him, Duggie? Did you get him?"

Duggie went as speechless as an Egyptian mummy.

"Well? Duggie? Speak to me!"

"See for yourself!" Duggie finally uttered.

Miserly Shakes rushed out the kennel door then through the kennel ground gate, followed by Duggie, who was now holding a net in his hand.

"Well I never!" exclaimed an elated Miserly Shakes. Slumped against the ground was a Golden Eagle with the dart pinned to one of its legs and Oscar wedged between the eagle and the cabin. Duggie quickly grabbed hold of Oscar and put him in the net, unlocked the cabin door and thrust Oscar out of the net onto the cabin floor. Miserly Shakes took the sedated eagle by its talons and carried it away to the enclosure that once was Oscar's, all the while feeling like he was in a dream which he could awake out of at any moment.

Witnessing this whole terrible episode, Jeremy flew back to the forest to inform the others. By the time Sebastian and Charlotte arrived with an army of forest birds, Oscar was shut in the cabin. Harry mustered the ranks of the Starlings together at the compound, but with the operation up in the air, their decoy was as effective as an army with paper swords. As Joey the "Pickpecker" was about to approach the cabin door, the unmistakable sound of the Hooded Crows from Dark Moor could be heard at the forest. Fearing their home and loved ones were under attack, they all hurried back.

The mood in the cabin had instantly reversed from ecstatic to gloomier than ever. Egbert, sensing Oscar's disappointment and despair, decided to intervene with some humour he only just managed to conjure up from the midst of his own personal sadness.

"Well, on the bright side," said Egbert, putting one of his large wings around his tiny friend, "whilst the accommodation at this hotel is appalling, the guests are pleasant, and the menu is just out of this world!"

# Don't give up!

Things in life don't always turn out how we **expect** them to. Life can be full of many disappointments, and even our most carefully put together plans can end up in disappointment and disaster. We may never know *what* the future holds, but it's good to know *Who* holds the future! When we surrender our life to God, and trust in the Lord Jesus Christ, we can be sure that whatever happens, good or ill, God has a purpose in it. And whatever God purposes, it is ultimately for our good and the blessing of others.

**"We know that all things work together for good to them that love God."** Romans 8:28

# Chapter 17
# Error

Miserly Shakes kept all three identical remote-controlled keys for his new magnetic door locks at the aviary, bundled together on a keyring, intending to give Duggie one of them, and to store the other one in his jar of spare things. The day had been long, commencing with the disaster of him falling in the mud swamp, thanks to his loose-as-a-cannon dog, Shanks. The excitement surrounding the capture of Oscar and the Golden Eagle helped to temporarily erase that misadventure from his mind. As he was about to put the sedated eagle in Oscar's old enclosure, he reached for his keys on his belt loop only to remember that he had forgotten to unclip them from his trousers that were muddied earlier - presently lying in the washing machine having undergone the most intensive programme the machine could offer.

"I thought you were at the enclosure," commented Duggie, wondering why his friend was coming out the cottage still holding the eagle his torch was presently shining on.

"Yeh … I … eh … forgot something," stammered Miserly Shakes, too embarrassed to tell Duggie what had happened. He quickly composed his thoughts again. "You should get yourself home, Duggie. You've got a busy day tomorrow, and you need to be at the Drumlachen Hotel as early as possible to drum up some interest with the tourists. Be sure to look your best."

"Aye, sure thing," replied Duggie, looking exceptionally pleased with himself with the capture of the two birds. "It's noon the gates open, isn't it?"

"Yip. I've a couple of helpers coming beforehand. I'll show them the ropes before I make myself scarce."

Duggie was about to head off when he heard a noise round by the cabin.

"Did you hear that, Sherrit? Sounded like activity outside the cabin."

"I suppose that'll be the Treecreeper you heard earlier, is it?" mocked Miserly. "Be off with you! I'll see to all this," he said, referring to the eagle and the birds in the cabin.

As Duggie's pickup truck clunked and rattled off, Miserly Shakes stood outside Oscar's old enclosure and, reaching for his keys, realised he'd forgotten again to give Duggie one of his spares. He shook his head and skewed his lips in annoyance with himself. Pointing one of the keys on the ring towards the enclosure door and pressing the button, nothing happened. After several further attempts it was clear the washing cycle had damaged it, as was the case with another key on the keyring. "Bother!" Miserly grumbled to himself. To his great relief, pressing the button of the remaining key made the lock buzz, causing it to demagnetise and allowing him a few seconds to open the enclosure door. Taking no chances, he jammed a stone to wedge the door ajar in case the key didn't work on his exit.

"Oh, they're going to love you, so they are," muttered Miserly to himself, as he put the eagle on the ground inside the enclosure. Little did he realise, however, that Duggie had made two mistakes that evening that would reverse their luck in the most spectacular fashion. In his excitement, Duggie had closed but not locked the cabin door where the birds were being held after he threw Oscar inside. The second mistake was more of an oversight, but would prove to be the most damaging to Miserly Shakes on a number of levels: the tranquilliser potion that was aimed at Oscar, but hit the Golden Eagle, was strong enough to sedate a small bird like a Northern Saw-whet Owl for a good length of time, but not a huge, strong bird like an eagle. As Miserly Shakes was about to leave the enclosure, the keys dangling in one of his hands and his torch in the other, the Golden Eagle slowly opened its eyes and fixed them on the strange-looking man with his back turned to it and the keys in his hand. Knowing what it had to do, it postured itself, ready to attack.

# Sin's consequences

We can all make mistakes and errors that we didn't mean to do, and many of them are harmless to ourselves and others, sometimes even very funny! The misspelling of my name as "Brain" instead of "Brian" on a number of messages I've received in the past, obviously wasn't intended as a compliment, it was just a simple typing **error**, and one which always makes me chuckle! What is more serious, however, is when we think, say or do things that we know are wrong. Very often, these things have a way of catching us out! Like a boomerang, they come back to us sooner or later.* All sin offends God, because God is holy and everything that is sinful is the opposite of who He is and what He takes pleasure in. Being a just and righteous God, means that He cannot just ignore or excuse our sin - He has to judge it! Wonderfully, the Lord Jesus paid the consequences of our sin on the cross to provide forgiveness for us. We come into the good of that great work Jesus did, when we simply place our trust in Him.

**"The wages of sin is death; but the gift of God is eternal life through Jesus Christ our Lord."** Romans 6:23

---

⚠ * "Whoever digs a pit will fall into it, and he who rolls a stone will have it roll back on him." Proverbs 26:27 (NKJV); "Be sure your sin will find you out." Numbers 32:23

# Chapter 18
# **Sacrifice**

Lying on the heather-covered ground in pitch darkness somewhere between Dark Moor and Mucklewood, Starandoff was surrounded by a murder of crows, the eldest nearest him, gaping at their long-time leader wondering if he'd ever recover.

Earlier that day, The Young Pretender was swept up into the grip of Virtos, the Golden Eagle, as the crow launched from the undergrowth to attack Sebastian and Charlotte. He told him about the Hoodies' plan to take over the forest before Virtos delivered the young upstart-of-a-crow to the birds of the forest, then left Mucklewood to go to Dark Moor. He encountered the Hooded Crows on route to Mucklewood and singled out Starandoff. A mighty swipe of his right wing on Starandoff's body set the leader of the Hoodies off balance. This was quickly followed up by a blunt strike to his head using his heavy beak, and some deep rips across Starandoff's flank and chest with his sharp talons. The old-timer had no chance against Virtos and nosedived from the sky like an aircraft shot down.

When the birds of the forest returned to their home following the failure of "Operation Flight", they discovered that their fear of the forest being invaded by the Hooded Crows was causeless. In fact, the noise they heard was from the captive Hoodies fighting among themselves - The Young Pretender being the centre point of the friction. Some of the Hoodies nearest the opening of an old badgers' sett, presently used to hold them captive, overheard the conversation of two Starlings concerning The Young Pretender. From what they understood, for Starlings are not easy to make out and very often talk over each other, The Young Pretender had betrayed them and was guilty of treachery against Starandoff. When challenged, The Young Pretender alleged that his accusers were making up lies for their own end. In no time, a division among the boisterous bunch arose and the Starlings extracted The Young Pretender from the midst of the clangorous scuffle before things got out of hand. The birds of the forest decided it best to set the cowardly crow free and to release the rest of the Hoodies some time after to make their way back to Dark Moor in the dark of night. The Young Pretender flew off in the opposite direction of Dark Moor, clearly not intending to return to the Dark Moor or Mucklewood any time soon.

Jeremy the Treecreeper had been trying to get the attention of the birds of the forest since their return, concerning something he forgot to mention about the capture of Oscar. His persistence finally paid off.

"It's about the Big Brown Bird," he said, addressing everyone. "I think it's on our side, I mean was on our side, or maybe still is - depends if it's alive or not!" His initial comments were met with expressions of confusion and pessimism, but Charlotte encouraged him to continue. "You see, I forgot to tell you exactly how Oscar came to being caught," he said, raising his voice to be heard over the Starlings who were arguing about Harry's unfitness to lead them on future missions. Incidentally, Harry held his ground quite admirably. "All I told you was the poacher put Oscar in a net and threw him in the cabin," continued Jeremy, "but if it wasn't for the Big Brown Bird, Oscar may have been killed. I think it may have sacrificed itself for Oscar." All the birds were silent now and attentive.

"What do mean?" asked Charlotte. "Are you saying that the Big Brown Bird has returned again?"

"Yes!" affirmed Jeremy. "It flew in the path of a sharp-pointed metal weapon with a feather on its end. It was clearly intended for Oscar, for there was one already fired that missed him and hit the cabin. I tried to warn Oscar, but everything happened so quickly. Whatever it was that hit the Big Brown Bird, it caused it to collapse to the ground before Miserly Shakes carried it away. The bird didn't put up any resistance and looked lifeless."

"Wait a minute!" intervened Sebastian. "That would explain something, would it not? What if it was the Big Brown Bird that dropped the crow from the sky?" he asked, referring to the express delivery of The Young Pretender earlier on.

Jeremy was emboldened to speak on. "Maybe the Big Brown Bird wasn't intending to attack us at the Walled Garden the day Charlotte was rescued after all," he suggested. "Perhaps it was just wanting to help."

"Oscar was right about it," stated Sebastian, remembering his little friend's words at the disused oil chamber, "and we had taken the Big Brown Bird for an enemy all along!"

The forest was now alive with bird debate, but everyone was unaware of the presence of those who had just arrived. Standing at a short distance behind them, about a stone's throw from the old Scots Pine, were eight birds enjoying their first taste of freedom since their captivity, and the ninth for his second!

# Lessons from Jesus' sacrifice

There have been many great sacrifices in the history of this world that we should never forget; like the many who fought and died in World War I & II in order to protect our country and the liberties we enjoy today. Perhaps you have a relation in your family history who sacrificed their life in one of those wars, and, if you have, I'm sure you're grateful for them. There is one sacrifice, however, that is more important than any other and has brought about the greatest freedom we can every know. I'm referring to the **sacrifice** Jesus made when He died in our place on the cross and the freedom He provided from the penalty of our sins* if we trust Him as our Saviour. Nothing can be added to that wonderful work; all we have to do is to trust in the Saviour! Are you trusting in Him? No! Then no better time to trust Him than now! Yes! Then you'll want to know how best to please Him. Some of the ways we can please the Lord Jesus is by having the same attitude He had to others and to God when He was here on the earth. By putting others before ourselves and giving more of our time to the things of God, we will be reflecting something of the life of the Lord Jesus Christ, for the glory and praise of God. A living sacrifice!

**"... present your bodies a living sacrifice, holy, acceptable unto God, which is your reasonable service."** Romans 12:1

———————

* "... Christ ... suffered once for sins, the just for the unjust, that He might bring us to God ..." 1 Peter 3:18 (NKJV)

# Chapter 19
# **Disappointment**

Of all the attractions that were offered to the tourists at Drumlachen Hotel, none were met with more enthusiasm than Mucklewood Aviary. Duggie, through the interpretation of Heidi, the local tour guide, was able to tell the foreign visitors that, as well as a Northern Saw-whet Owl, they had just acquired a new addition to the aviary. Hoping to persuade any who were in two minds about going, he assured them that this addition would not disappoint any viewers, whether or not they were bird enthusiasts.

With all the publicity surrounding the reopening of the aviary, a fledgling reporter from a regional newspaper and local to the area was asked to attend the opening. The editor of the newspaper wasn't expecting anything more from him than perhaps a couple of paragraphs in a column to use as a filler, with a picture to accompany the small article - if they had space to squeeze it in. Danny, the young reporter, was an old school friend of Heidi and happily agreed to tag along with her as she guided the tourists to the various attractions; starting off with the Winter Gardens after breakfast, Mucklewood Aviary following lunch, and finally a visit to The Old Mill House where the visitors from China could enjoy some late afternoon refreshments.

Delighted with the Winter Gardens, the mood amongst the tourists for their next stop was one of excitement and anticipation. However, everything seemed eerily quiet when the large group entered the compound. Duggie, noticing that no one was manning the ticket office, muttered some words of disdain about the unreliability of youths and shuffled through the bottlenecked crowd at the narrow entrance point. He took all the payments - advertised well in advance as "cash only" - before allowing each visitor past the gate to where Heidi was waiting for them holding a small hand-drawn map of the aviary grounds which Duggie had given to her.

Standing outside the cabin where the birds had been temporarily kept, Heidi gave a few notices about what they could expect to see and restated, as Duggie asked her to, that there was a "mystery addition" to the aviary which was sure to impress. The cabin door where the birds were temporarily held was wide open and the dart which missed Oscar was still lodged in the wooden panel, much to the curiosity of Danny, the newspaper reporter. Heidi led the way towards the west wing where, according to the map on the guide, they were supposed to encounter an Ivory-Billed Aracari in the first enclosure, a Nightjar in the second, a Saw-whet Owl in the third (intended last minute to be moved there to allow for the Golden Eagle to occupy Oscar's old enclosure) and then a Hoopoe bird in the corner enclosure.

By the time the company had reached the fourth enclosure, Duggie, still at the ticket office, could hear the clamour of voices and peeped his head out the window. Heavy and unforgiving frowns were worn on many of the visitors' faces; hands were gesturing all over the place, like a conference of confused traffic controllers, and some were rubbing their thumbs along their fingers intimating that they wanted their money back. He had no idea what they were saying, but one thing was clear to him - they weren't at all impressed. Puzzled as to why, but not at all inclined to engage with the cheerless crowd, Duggie grabbed the money box and shot off in his Pickup truck like he had just entered the last lap of a rally race.

"If you could all calm down please," appealed Heidi in Mandarin. "I'm sure there's a perfectly logical explanation for this." She had just witnessed Duggie speeding off in his truck and only hoped by the time they ventured round the corner, to where the "mystery bird" and the Shoebill Stork were to be, that at least these birds would be in their enclosures. So far, none of the other birds were! To their amazement, the forest-facing middle enclosure was occupied. Sitting down on the dirt, with his head tucked in-between his knees and his hands clasped on the back of his head, sat Miserly Shakes in the locked enclosure. Danny grabbed for his camera to capture the scene, preferring the portrait orientation over landscape, allowing him to frame in the caption of the banner that was hanging over the enclosure: 'We Care for the Rare!' Danny had just scooped up his first story, and it was a big one!

The visitors followed Danny's lead and in no time compact cameras and smartphones were snapping pictures, as tourists do, of this once-in-a-lifetime photo opportunity. They had encountered a "rare" creature indeed, but far less majestical than the one they had anticipated!

At length, the police arrived and ushered the visitors out of the compound, assuring them that they would all be refunded back at the hotel. Miserly Shakes couldn't believe the misfortunes of that day. A little girl took pity on him and poured out the contents of her purse - three foreign coins - into the donations box outside the enclosure. She said something to him in Mandarin, but Miserly was too lost in his own world of misery to take any notice of her. Heidi's face broke into a smile as the little girl skipped along to rejoin her parents. "Don't be sad, lonely big bird," Heidi said to Danny, interpreting the little girl's words for him.

# Who can we look to?

The "profiteroles with chocolate sauce" option had my name written all over it. This was the one that stood out of the dessert menu as the obvious choice; the others hardly got so much as a second glance from me. However, when the profiteroles were served with *cold* chocolate sauce - something that should never, ever, be done - my heart sank and I couldn't help but pay more attention to the other desserts on the table. "Serves you right for ignoring us," they all seemed to be saying to me.

When people or things don't live up to what we expect them to it can be very disappointing indeed. Even those who profess to be Christians can **disappoint** us and may cause us to become discouraged in our own Christian faith. Look even closer, and you will discover that there have been times when you have disappointed yourself, never mind others! Best to look away from ourselves and others to the One who never disappoints - Jesus Christ!

**"Jesus Christ the same yesterday, and today, and for ever."**
Hebrews 13:8

# Oscar's Wings

# Chapter 20
# **Delight**

The previous evening, Virtos had dealt with Miserly Shakes with the same efficiency and effectiveness as he had with the old oil chamber lid, The Young Pretender, and Starandoff. With Miserly's back to him, he leapt onto his head, grabbed two clumps of his long straggly hair with his talons and spun him round and round, causing him to feel as if he was on some horrific horseless merry-go-round! When Vitros finally released him, the latest dizzy and disorientated victim of the great eagle staggered then floppped to the ground like he had been struck a knockout blow in a boxing match. Virtos grabbed the remote controlled keys which fell to the ground away from Miserly Shakes and flew out of the door, dislodging the stone used as a door wedge on his way out - the door locking shut behind him. He flew off in the direction from which he came to Mucklewood that day, dropping the keys in an expanse of scrubby wasteland.

To the delight of the birds of Mucklewood forest, Oscar was back once more at the old Scots Pine, not just in presence, but back in his animated story-telling mode, accompanied either side of him by his friends of the aviary.

As Oscar unfolded how they escaped, Egbert, completely exhausted with all of the evening's drama, fell deep into sleep where he stood.

"Unknown to us at the time, the cabin door was unlocked!" Oscar explained, shaking his head and gesturing with his wings to indicate his disbelief at Duggie's carelessness. "Frustrated with how things turned out," Oscar continued, "Egbert collapsed against the door and ended doing a backward flip out to the yard."

At that precise point during Oscar's account, Egbert collapsed on his side with a huge thump followed by him bellowing out: "Surrender!" - presumably something to do with what he had just been dreaming about! The timing was impeccable and instantly prompted a surge of laughter among all the birds before Oscar was able to resume again.

Oscar finished his speech by thanking the birds of the forest for their attempt to set him and his captive friends of the aviary free.

"You may think 'Operation Flight' was a disaster," he said, "but you'd be wrong! You have all proved to us without any question that you are the type of friends worth having. No! ..." he paused briefly for effect, "... You're more than friends to us, you are family!"

Just then, a bird not unlike Oscar but slightly larger, emerged from a hole in a tree behind him. With a few flaps of its weak and tired wings it took up position next to Oscar. Fran, the Raven, looked uneasy in its presence and slunk into the darkness and cover of the foliage behind her, as betrayers do.

"That's my boy," the other owl said, addressing Oscar.

Instantly, and to his amazement and delight, Oscar recognised the voice he had stored and replayed as a soothing echo in his mind during most of his young life until now.

"Mother!"

**THE END**

# The Father's delight

Every proud parent thinks there's no one quite like their kids. In truth, there has only ever lived One perfect Person. When God looked down from heaven upon the earth He created,* we are told in the Bible that everyone had gone astray after their own heart** - God had been left out of their lives and thinking; how sad! There was a day, however, when God spoke from heaven and announced His **delight** in His Son.*** The Lord Jesus was just about to commence His service to God in a public way before the nation of Israel, and as God looked back on thirty years since His Son left heaven and came into the world - born in Bethlehem's manger - He rejoiced that His Son had brought nothing but pleasure to Him. Try as we may, we cannot bring any delight to God by our own efforts. When we trust the Lord Jesus and what He has done for us on the cross, however, because God is so pleased with His Son and all He has done, we are accepted through Christ and brought into God's family.

**"For by grace you have been saved through faith, and that not of yourselves; it is the gift of God, not of works, lest anyone should boast."** Ephesians 2:8-9 (NKJV)

---

 * "In the beginning God created the heavens and the earth." Genesis 1:1 (NKJV)

 ** "And God saw that the wickedness of man was great in the earth, and that every imagination of the thoughts of his heart was only evil continually." Genesis 6:5

 *** "And Jesus, when He was baptised, went up straightway out of the water: and, lo, the heavens were opened unto Him, ... and lo a voice from heaven, saying, 'This is My beloved Son, in whom I am well pleased.'" Matthew 3:16-17

133

# Oscar's Wings

# Epilogue

"Well, well. Look what we have here," snarled one of the foxes from the Lachen skulk. It was roaming alone around the perimeter of Mucklewood forest, looking for prey.

"An injured owl. I say, what a poor fellow!"

The owl lay still and helpless on the heather-covered ground, rigid with fear.

"I know exactly what to do with you," the fox said.

Before the owl knew it, the fox had him vice-gripped in its mouth and carried him away to his earth near the village of Drumlachen.

"I came so close. So close!" muttered the owl to himself in despair. "Now I shall never see my son, Oscar, again."

Crossing a shallow burn and moving cautiously in the open spaces, as foxes do, it finally arrived at the territory of the Lachens and placed its catch down on the wild-grown grass.

In no time, the others congregated, following the lead of Darvic, the dominant male.

"Good work," said Darvic, commending his cousin. "Bring her!" he ordered back to the earth. "Now we shall see where her loyalties lie: with the Lachens or the Muckles."

A young vixen was accompanied out of the earth by two older vixens at her side and a young tod behind her.

"Not much of a meal," remarked Darvic, referring to the owl and directing his remark to the young vixen, "but it will do on this occasion. His life, or yours!"

The young vixen knew what she had to do. She had no other choice. As she approached the owl the other foxes retreated back and encircled both of them. She put her mouth to its body and, lifting her head slightly, fixed her eyes on Trex, the young tod.

Oscar's father closed his eyes tight, anticipating the inevitable.

"NOW!" yelped one of the older vixens.